Off The Rack

LIANA BROOKS

OTHER WORKS

HEROES AND VILLAINS

Even Villains Fall In Love
Even Villains Go To The Movies
Even Villains Have Interns
Even Villains Play The Hero (books 1 – 3
omnibus)

TIME AND SHADOWS MYSTERIES

The Day Before
Convergence Point
Decoherence

FLEET OF MALIK

Bodies In Motion
Change of Momentum (forthcoming)
For Every Action (forthcoming)

Find other works by the author at
www.lianabrooks.com

Off The Rack

INKLET #2

LIANA BROOKS

Inkprint PRESS

www.inkprintpress.com

Print ISBN: 978-1-925825-02-2
eBook ISBN: 9781386102991

www.inkprintpress.com

*National Library of Australia Cataloguing-in-Publication
Data*
Liana Brooks 1982 –
Off The Rack
54 p.
ISBN: 978-1-925825-02-2
Inkprint Press, Canberra, Australia
1. Fiction—Short Stories 2. Fiction—Science
Fiction 3. Fiction—Science Fiction—Humorous

First Print Edition: January 2019
Cover design © Inkprint Press
Interior art © Amy Laurens

OFF THE RACK

THE SOLUTION TO LISA'S PROBLEM glowed neon in the fading light. She pulled into the parking lot under the sign with words blinking "Free Groom Half Price Ring Bearer w/ Every Wedding Gown".

Inside, the boutique was softly lit. No crass racks of squashed satin dresses here. Elegant confections of lace, pearl, and silk each stood center spotlight in a variety of wedding vistas.

One gown, a simple silk design, was advertised as the best for a beach wedding, the price for beach and horses thoughtfully included on the price tag. Another gown looked like the work of a deranged fairy godmother with some magpie in her ancestry, and was touted as ideal for a themed Cinderella wedding.

Lisa browsed until she caught the clerk's attention.

"I'm so sorry you had to wait, Miss. I was just seeing to another happy customer. Now, which dress were you looking at?"

"I rather like the beach dress—" Lisa began.

"A favorite theme," the clerk interrupted, nodding enthusiastically. "Very chic this season."

Lisa pulled an indecisive face. "Yes, but the train doesn't quite suit me."

"If you can describe what you want, I can point you in the direction of several lovely gowns. Or I can show you some of our recent arrivals?"

"Something figure-hugging, but not trashy." Lisa sketched an hourglass shape in the air with her hands. "I want to go for understated taste and old-world elegance. Maybe a few pearls or a touch of crystal. Nothing ostentatious though."

A pad of paper had appeared from nowhere and the clerk took detailed notes with quick glides of her pen. "Would you prefer a pure white or an ivory?"

"Pure white. This is my first wedding, I want to do it properly."

"Of course. Don't we all?" The clerk's head bobbed like a chicken as she focused on her notes. "What kind of sleeve were you looking for?"

"Sleeveless. For a summer wedding."

The clerk nodded once more, a decisive gesture. "Something drapey, long, and sleeveless. You know, I think I have just the gown. It might be your size too. It's an Elyia, and we were only able to get three of her gowns this year. A little pricey..."

There was a judicious pause.

"Money is not an issue," Lisa assured her.

"Perfect." The clerk beamed happily. "The gown is pure silk, a mermaid silhouette, you know. It hugs and then flares below the knee. Very artistic. No embellishments, but I know it will be perfect for you."

And it was. Lisa twirled in front of the three-way mirror. Cool silk swirled around her ankles. Curves she didn't know she had popped into place and gave her the kind of figure women usually paid surgeons big money for.

"I'll take it!"

"Excellent." The clerk glowed. "I'll write it up for you."

Lisa changed in the dressing room and handed the gown over to a hovering underling. "Now," Lisa said to the clerk, smiling. "About the groom..."

"Right this way, please." Still humming, the clerk led Lisa past fantasy wedding settings, rows of hothouse flowers set in stasis and perfect for everything from boutonnieres to bouquets, and into a back room. She flicked on a light.

Rows of grooms hung awkwardly with coat hooks down the back of their tuxedos.

Some were so short their feet dangled several inches above the floor; others were so tall that they sat folded up. To one side, the plus-sized grooms circled slowly on a rack like a herd of tethered balloons.

"Ignore the tuxedos," the clerk said, straightening the tie on a short groom propped on a display rack. His feet kicked a few inches above the ground as he mumbled in his sleep. "Clothes are interchangeable. So are the shoes." The clerk turned. "Did you have something already in mind? Off the rack, maybe? Or did you want a custom groom?"

Lisa clicked her tongue in thought. "I really don't know. I've never been groom shopping before. What do you advise?"

"Why don't you have a look around and check the tags while I get you some refreshments? You've already been in the store over an hour. Shopping makes one hungry."

"Tea and biscuits?"

"Don't be silly!" the clerk said, horrified. "For groom shopping we have chocolate-dipped strawberries and champagne."

Lisa smiled gratefully. "That sounds delightful."

While the clerk bustled out in search of a light repast, Lisa browsed the aisles of grooms. Most of the men slept. A few mumbled to each other, and one winked at her in a coquettish manner.

She checked the tag on one of the folded grooms while he snored with a cute snuffle.

Name: Todd
Personality: Deferential
Height: 6'5"
Weight: 215 lb
Age: 29
Income: $56,750 annually

Lisa flipped the tag over to catch the care details. Self-washing, cooked 70% of his meals, but required special weekend care in the form of regular poker nights out with the boys. She frowned.

"Oh," the clerk said, coming back with a little trolley. "You don't want that one. Those models are best for second marriages and planned divorces. The seams tend to loosen up after a few years and they balloon." She gave an apologetic smile. "We have a strict No Return policy on grooms."

"Right." Lisa let the tag drop.

"What do you like?" the clerk asked.

"I'm leaning to the taller ones. Something to make me look a little less rangy."

"Do you prefer athletic or thin, dear?" With a practiced eye the clerk started pulling grooms off the rack. She held up two specimens, one with the heavy muscled look common in football players and the other a reedy fellow with glasses slipping off his nose.

"Muscular, but not that bulky. I don't want him to make me look fat."

The clerk nodded. "I wouldn't say anything, of course, but so many girls come in here and pick grooms that don't suit their look at all. They forget a husband is an accessory you wear every day, and treat it like dress shopping. You need to take the long view. Your dress only has to look good once, but a groom needs to retain shape for months. Years, in some extreme cases! Here, try this one." The clerk held out a lithe man with good muscle tone, blond hair cut short, and a steady in-and-out type of snore.

Lisa checked the tag while the clerk unfolded the sleeping man. "Isn't he a little long for me? The tag says six foot eight. I'm only five seven."

"A little shorter then?"

She hesitated, scanning the tag. "I don't know. Can you do alterations? Maybe take an inch or two off the legs?"

"Not with these ones. But we do have the custom-fit grooms in the next room." The clerk folded the unwanted groom up and placed him back on the rack. "All the grooms are free with the gown purchase. Custom is as cheap as off-the-rack today, so you might as well get what you like."

"You're right." Lisa smiled. "Let's go look at the custom designs then."

The clerk led her into a blue-lit room filled with vats and situated her in a comfortable chair in front of a large screen with the trolley of food next to it.

Lisa sipped her champagne as the clerk turned on the computer. Bubbles rippled through the vat nearest her, making the lone leg turn in its nutrient broth.

"Now, here," the clerk said. "You can program in all the parameters. The basic hair and eye color are very easy to change later if you want, but after the groom is altered we can't change metabolism, personality, or height. So be very sure that you enter those correctly."

The list wasn't as endless as it first seemed. Lisa entered her preferences on the right of the screen and the computer displayed her potential groom on the left. She selected the advanced options and dithered over setting his income. "If I give him a high income will he be gone too much, do you think?"

The clerk shrugged. "It depends on what occupation you choose for him. That's right down there, question twelve. You can set a very high income if you choose the right profession. And heirs are usually very indolent, always at home. But they also have the highest percentage of thefts in the nation. You don't want someone to sneak in and steal your groom on the wedding night."

Bitter memories twisted Lisa's features. "No. I don't."

She selected an income of $96,560 annually, more than enough when combined with her own salary, and a profession as a college professor. She turned to the clerk. "Will I need to pay extra for his education?"

"Usually, but not with our current special. The wedding season is almost over and we honestly need to move these older models out. The ones I can't sell will go to the government. At a discount, of course," the clerk hastened to add, lest she seem unpatriotic.

Lisa nodded, not really listening. "The computer wants to know a percentage for fertility. How do I calculate that? Is it so many times out of ten we get pregnant, or so many times out of ten we don't?"

"The fertility percentage is per time. Women have a much lower fertility rate, usually not over twenty-five percent, so you want his correspondingly high. Eighty-five to ninety-five is the fashionable level at the moment. You could put it higher if you want more children or at zero if you aren't interested in having them the old fashioned way. It won't affect the groom's performance at all."

"Right." She set the fertility percentage at ninety and moved on to a question about social skill-sets. Did she want a pre-set personality or to mix and match her own?

The clerk refilled her glass. "Would you like a ring bearer today too? They're half price."

Lisa glanced up. "Oh! I hadn't even looked. Really, I always thought I'd have a flower girl. Do you sell those?"

"Only the dresses. But we do have an arrangement with the local modeling and acting agency. If you buy bridesmaid and flower girl dresses here, they'll give you seventy-five percent off the cost of renting a bridal party."

She nodded. "I might look into that."

"If you choose one of their pre-posed parties I already have the sizes on file, so you won't need to come in and actually meet with the bridal party before the wedding. We find some brides prefer that."

Lisa bunched her lips in thought. "Hmmm. I do have some friends. I'll have to talk to them and see if they're interested in coming to the wedding. Everyone's so busy lately, it's hard to get people to take the time off work."

"Bring pictures to the modeling agency and let them find look-alikes for the wedding," the clerk suggested. "That way your girlfriends can be there without actually wasting any of their own time."

Lisa nodded and hit the last button. "There. That's my groom!"

The clerk looked over her selections. "Oh! Isn't he handsome? An excellent choice. You have exquisite taste. He'll look fabulous next to you.

Now, you do know that the custom-made grooms aren't ready to go today? It will take three weeks for the order to get in. You weren't planning on having the wedding this week, were you?"

Lisa shook her head. "No. I was thinking a summer wedding in a few months."

"Good. Good. Did you want to pick the groom up beforehand or the day of? Remember, you can't return him once he leaves the store. If you think you might get cold feet it's best to leave him in our vault until the day of the wedding. You can always call us up and tell us you've changed your mind. We'll put him out on the rack for a twenty-five dollar restocking fee."

"That sounds good. I'll pick him up the day of."

"Excellent." The clerk gestured to a door. "Would you like to look over our ring bearer selection?"

"Certainly."

The ring bearers were in a smaller room combining both racks of small boys and several smaller vats. All the ring bearers were sleeping fitfully.

"We have one of the largest selections of ring bearers in the city," the clerk said. "You have your choice of ages, from toddler through teenager. And we have the Grow Your Own option. It's very popular for people who choose Living in Sin before marriage. You can take both the prospective groom and the infant ring bearer home on the same day with a voucher. When the ring bearer has reached the size you want you just bring in the voucher and we'll fit him to a suit."

Peering curiously into the vat where a pair of feet led their own private existence until needed, Lisa asked, "Is that a popular choice?"

"Very popular. People love to have their own screaming brat carrying their ring down the aisle. It makes for such a cute video and, of course, the wedding reception fight always needs a good screaming brat."

Lisa shook her head. "I don't know. I never really wanted a son."

"Then why not consider our rental options?" The clerk motioned to a rack of freckle-faced boys labeled 'six-year olds'. "We call this the nephew option, although you don't need to buy an Aunt or Uncle with them. We lease them to you for a twenty-four hour period and with the proper application of sugar they can be very good."

"Well. I just..."

"Or maybe the teenage nephew?" The clerk bustled Lisa over to another rack where gawky teens hung in ill-fitted suits. "These models have the full range of sarcastic comments, insults, and eye-rolling. Although a well applied fifty will keep them from making hurtful remarks or hitting on your maid of honor."

"Gosh, I just don't know," Lisa said fretfully.

"There's no rush," the clerk assured her. "Our sale doesn't end until Friday. That gives you plenty of time to plan out the details and coordinate with the wedding planner. Just bring the receipt for the gown in when you come back during our sale period and you can have whatever you like."

"Perfect." Lisa collected her gown and voucher for her new groom.

Back at home, she wrote out wedding invitations and wondered how her foremothers had handled all these messy complications. What did you do if you woke up one morning and wanted to marry before they invented bridal shops with everything you needed?

Probably relied on dating. As if that ever worked!

She took extra care in addressing the invitation to Michael and Janie. Let her ex and her ex-best friend see just how hurt she was by his dumping her: Not at all!

Janie could have her off-the-rack boyfriend with his part-time job. She was getting herself a real man.

THE MAKING OF
OFF THE RACK

Where did this start?

On a dusty road, in front of a fading store front, on a chalk sign that read "Everything You Need For Your Wedding! Half off!"

It was in the rural south, somewhere between Texas and Alabama, in a place with Spanish moss and lace and cicadas singing in the heat.

Wouldn't it be funny, I thought, if the sign were true. Wouldn't it be nice if you could walk into a shop and order everything you needed for a wedding, from a spouse, to the dress, to the supportive family?

...Well? Wouldn't it?

DOWNLOAD YOUR FREE EBOOK

When you buy a print book from Inkprint Press, we like to say THANK YOU by offering you the ebook for free!

Please head to www.inkprintpress.com/inklets/2/ and the use the coupon INKLET2 to get your copy of this Inklet in epub AND mobi today!
(Coupon will only work once.)

Read more by Liana Brooks!

BODIES IN MOTION
CHAPTER ONE

THE PROBLEM WITH VACATIONS, Selena reflected as she adjusted her sweater outside Cargo Blue, was that reality was always waiting at the end. A quick search of the local security cameras found one that showed the peeling sunburn on her right shoulder blade.

Such was the curse of pale-skinned, ship-born Fleet personnel. Anytime she left the foggy belts covering the city of Tarrin, she barbecued like a shrimp, no matter how much sunscreen she applied. Otherwise, she'd flee even further from the Fleet Enclave and make her home on the equatorial beaches of the planet they were trapped on.

She panned the camera and checked her left shoulder. Black ink made a starscape that disguised three silver scars as shooting stars. The painting covered her shoulder blade and part of her upper arm. As the artist had promised, the skin-paint had kept her from burning as much, though it still had the over-stretched feel of a burn. With a few adjustments, her uniform covered most of the temporary art; it would keep her from having to explain to her colleagues.

Her forearm warmed, a warning that someone was about to contact her through the tech implant tucked between her radius and ulna.

She hesitated too long and the call came through, a persistent ping against her skull as the phantom image of her best friend floated on the edge of her vision.

Selena turned off the visual receiver and answered. "Genevieve," she said with a smile as the image of her vivacious, red-headed friend appeared floating against the backdrop of landing gear that supported the grounded fleet.

A grounder would have thought she was talking to herself, but grounders wouldn't set foot near the neo-city-state of Enclave. The rocky beach served as a city and tomb for the sur-vivors of the last war.

"Selena!" Gen gushed. "Starcom to Selena. Where are you? I'm covering for now."

"Delayed, but almost there." Selena hoped Gen wouldn't hear the lie. She'd been standing in the shadows of the Enclave pub for nearly a quarter hour.

"The *Lorenza* could get here faster," Gen said, referencing a long-dead ship whose crew were found skeletonized at their stations. Gen blew hair off her face. "Stars above, you're an hour late. The whole fleet is flying faster than you."

Selena turned on her visual long enough to roll her eyes at her friend.

"Ha, ha, funny. That joke needs to be forcibly retired." Sooner rather than later. The fleet couldn't fly without fuel, and the Malik system they were stranded in held precious few deposits of the orun crystals needed to power the ships.

"If you don't come," Gen said threateningly, "I will teleport to your apartment and drag you out in your pajamas."

"I'm not at home," Selena admitted. And she wouldn't have let her best friend come to her new house if she was.

Gen was smart enough to realize that the small palace Selena had bought in downtown Tarrin wasn't paid for by her official OIA salary. The paygrades for the Office of Imperial Affairs had last been updated when the Malik system was still in contact with the empire, making them 900 years out of date.

Technically, taking a second job wasn't treason, but there were enough people in the fleet who'd see it as a betrayal that keeping it secret felt right. Especially since Gen's captain was one who would scream the loudest.

Gen clapped. "Selena! Stop stalling yer engines and get in here. This isn't some Fleet Tribunal, just our friends. You, me, Carver. I left a message for Marshall. You know. People we like."

The light of understanding dawned. "Carver? This is so you can snuggle up to Perrin Carver without your parents watching?"

"Yes," Gen admitted, not looking the least bit contrite.

"You're only dragging me along so I can cover for you while you make out in a corner, aren't you?" She masked the relief with mock anger. At least Gen wasn't trying to set Selena up with one of her cousins.

Or, ancestors forbid, Gen's handsy older brother.

Again.

Gen opened her eyes wide with an innocent smile. "Maybe."

"Gen!" Selena rolled her eyes. "Doesn't he have his own place?"

"Just the bachelor's dorm. The Carvers didn't have any ships except the shuttle his parents crashed in. Making out next door to Mom and Dad? No. And the BOQ? It's so tacky. You can hear everything through those walls."

Selena hid a smile. "I'll be there soon enough."

If Gen ever caught wind of how panicky the thought of a relationship made her, Gen would make it her life's goal to see Selena paired off. And there wasn't a man alive who she could imagine getting close to now.

Her implant helpfully pulled up an image of a tall, broad-shouldered, lean-muscled fighter with skin black as the night between stars and emerald-green eyes.

She pushed the memory away.

Lieutenant Commander Titan Sci-arra was striking, intelligent, and had a body she'd cross battle lines for, but he was also out of reach. There was no point in chasing a man who wouldn't give her the time of day.

Another crew shuffled past her into the bar, black patches with silver fists on their shoulders.

It was getting harder to pretend she belonged in Enclave, with the fleet. Once upon a time, she'd known every crew's patch without thinking. She could name captains, their ships and their seconds by rote. Now she would need to tap into the fleet's information nexus if she wanted to know who they were.

She stopped at the edge of the door to tug her lightest shields into place. A few minor adjustments would keep bugs away, keep beer off her clothes, and prevent anyone from hacking into her implant. They could still send messages, because disallowing that would have raised eyebrows. And they could still hit her. But she could always hit back.

Selena rolled her shoulders and strutted into Cargo Blue. It was a battlefield, but she was the last captain of the Caryll family, and she wasn't going down without a fight.

Whatever crew owned Cargo Blue probably hadn't had much of a decorating budget, but at least they'd stuck with a theme: oversized cargo boxes were piled up to make walls, seating, and tables. Olive-green safety webbing draped from the ceiling between blue lights. Fog used for fire drills on the ships pumped across the floor to hide the concrete beneath.

There was no bouncer at the door,

but people were still hanging around the entrance.

As a rule, the fleet was cautious, and the young faces she saw belonged to fleet members who had never ventured outside their own crew more than a few times, even though the fleet had been grounded for nearly three years.

Tables to the left, bar ahead, dance floor to the right… and that meant the back half of the cargo hanger had been partitioned and karaoke would be in the back right corner. After a few minutes of weaving through the human crush, she found Gen, already sitting in Perrin Carver's lap and giggling.

"Selena!" Gen jumped up and hugged her. "I was beginning to worry!"

"How many people are in here?" Selena shouted over the music.

"Everyone under forty?" Gen laughed. With a small hand wave Gen put up a minor sound shield, muting the music. "People are going to stir crazy. Combine that with the anniversary—"

The anniversary.

Today.

The day the war had begun, the day the united fleet had died.

They'd been dying for four hundred years, well aware that the reserve of orun crystals was depleted and there was no way to move forward with the ships they had.

Old Captain Baular had seen the deposit of orun on the fifth planet as their saving grace. He'd get it even if it meant killing the grounders. And, coward that he was, he'd ordered his grandson to lead the first attack instead of leading it himself.

That opening skirmish began and ended in the dark, with Titan Sciarra in the infirmary, and five Academy fighters missing or damaged. But by lunch of the next day, every officer belonging to crews allied with the Baulars withdrew.

Seven months later, heated words turned to live rounds.

"Selena?" Gen asked quietly, placing a hand on her arm. "You didn't know the date, did you?"

"I was trying not to think about." If she had, she'd have cut her vacation to the islands early. Maybe even made her pilgrimage to the small cay where she'd ditched her stolen fighter after driving off the attack.

She rolled her shoulder, stretching the deep scars. "It snuck up on me."

"First round, we drink to the Lost Fleet, and all who've gone on to crew it. I'm buying," Gen said with a touch of forced joviality. "Carver's been making friends. Tell her, babe." She pushed Carver's shoulder.

Perrin Carver was tall, broad-shouldered man with shy, hazel eyes that hid a wicked sense of humor.

Selena's heart fluttered just a little at the memory of a time when she'd fancied herself in love with him. He'd been the ideal starsider: intelligent, good-looking, and charismatic.

They'd been friends of a sort, but even that relationship had soured when she'd realized he'd been getting close to her so he could learn more about Genevieve Silar.

Carver nodded and held out his hand. "Hi, Selena. How are you?"

She tapped the back of his hand with hers, letting him test her shields. "Good. How's the Starguard?"

"Booming." The commander of the Star-guard smiled, white teeth flashing, but there was a tightness around his eyes. "Everyone hears about guardians being allowed outside the Enclave, or working with the Jhandarmi, and I'm drowning in recruiting requests. Captains of larger crews invite me to Captain's Mess so they can introduce me to their best and brightest. Half the time I can't tell if they want me to marry into the crew or take the fleetlings into the guard." His shield was still attached to hers, scanning her as he talked.

All he would get from her was polite interest. Her heartrate didn't spike or dip at the mention of the Jhandarmi. Her smile never flickered.

"Maybe you should lock down Gen," Selena said. "If you had a spouse, no one would try to get you to marry into the crew."

Carver and Gen shared a look, and Gen sent a ping of information that Selena's implant translated as an ongoing debate over crew name and a place to live.

Carver sent something similar; a picture of his bachelor's quarters and his one ship.

There was no room for them to marry and have a family.

"Enclave is a temporary solution," Selena said out loud. She'd lost the taste for communicating by implant years ago. "If we—"

A heavy hand wrapped around her waist as someone wearing too much cologne stepped far too close to her. "Hello, Selena."

Hollis Silar, one of Gen's many siblings, kissed her temple.

Simultaneously, Selena sighed, sent a shock through her shield to Hollis's hand, and el-bowed him in the gut. "Hi, Hollis. I see you're still bathing in cologne rather than water."

He stepped away from her, an easy smile still in place.

It wasn't that Hollis was bad looking; plenty of women found him handsome. It was that he was equally affectionate with every woman he saw and he couldn't keep a secret to save his life. Or anyone else's. He'd chase anyone with a pretty smile and fell in and out of love a couple of times a day.

"Nice to see you too, Selena. Now, everyone, you're all going to look at me, smile, and laugh like I'm my normal, dashing self," he said, his smile never changing. "You haven't been paying attention, but I'm not a member of the Star-guard for nothing. We're being watched. Now take your nice drinks from the waitress and keep your eyes on me."

Hollis nodded to the waitress and handed out four cups with bright purple liquid. "Bruised Stars all around. Guaranteed to make you giggle, or so the guy at the bar told me. Although he's a Seutaai, so take it with a shield in place." He handed Selena her drink with a smile, but turned immediately to glance over his shoulder.

"Big brother, who are we looking for?" Gen asked with a slow drawl. "Is it a friend who you might have forgotten to call back after a night out?"

Hollis shook his head. "No, I thought I saw some of the Lee crew. Make that, I'm certain of it."

Selena grimaced. "As long as Rowena isn't here."

"Did you call me?"

Startled, Selena looked up to the face of her least favorite woman: Rowena Lee. "Hello," Selena said politely. "I see you're still alive. That's…" *Unfortunate.* She nodded and took a slug of her Bruised Star.

Rowena held up a tray of electric blue shots. "My crew thinks I can't out-drink anyone in this bar. I probably can't go toe-to-toe with alcoholics like the Silars here. But No-Shot Selena?" Rowena set the drinks on the table. "I can out-shoot you in the stars or on the ground."

Gen sucked in air between her teeth and sent Selena several urgent pings telling her to ignore the Lees.

Selena muted Gen. "I took plenty of shots in the war. As I recall, I disabled three of your big birds. *Bassi, Aryton, Theoano…* Bang, bang, bang." Selena mimed firing with her finger. "Three shots. Three silent ships."

"Not kills," Rowena said. "A whole war and you never blooded yourself."

That was it, the memory she didn't want to face; the time she'd almost taken Death's claim and risked killing someone outside of war.

"That's uncalled for," Hollis said, trying to step between them. "Selena, why don't we—"

Selena pushed Hollis aside and grabbed the first shot.

She tossed back the potent drink and shattered the glass on the table. "Go suck vacuum, Rowena. You're a pissant yeoman with no hope of command."

"I went to the Academy, same as you, Selena. I fought for the fleet." Rowena slammed a shot back. "You fought for the mud-lickers."

Selena took another shot as the first started to fuzz her judgement. "I prevented the Baulars from committing mass genocide and destroying the civilians along with the fleet."

Rowena took her second shot. A crowd was gathering and that seemed to feed her cruelty. "The Lees survived the war. We're still here. How many Caryll captains are there? Oh, right, one. Can you count that high, No-Shot? You have any idea how easy it would be for me to end you right now?"

Selena took the last two glasses and slammed them both back.

Gen pinged her, giving locations,

counts, and identities of the Lee allies in the crowd.

Hollis stepped to her flank, ready to defend her.

She stood, anger burning through her veins. "Sure, your crew outnumbers mine. I guess on paper, it's not really a fair fight, is it, Rowena? But you were trained as a flight leader, and what do Carylls do? Hand-to-hand combat. Maybe I should thin your ranks, starting with one mouthy yeoman."

Keep reading! Head to:
<u>http://www.lianabrooks.com/</u>
<u>bodies-in-motion/</u>
to buy your copy now!

ABOUT THE AUTHOR

LIANA BROOKS has never been off her home planet, but she hopes that one day NASA will call her up and offer her the job as writer-in-residence for any mission going anywhere. It sounds like fun.

Until that happy day, she can be found busily inventing new worlds for science fiction fans to explore in her study in the Pacific Northwest.

She has written the popular *Time and Shadows Mysteries* series about clones and the dangers of time travel; the *Fleet of Malik* series of connected sci-fi romances about re-building after a decades long war; and the cult-following *Heroes and Villains* series of superhero romances.

You can find out more about Liana at her website, www.lianabrooks.com.

INKLETS

Collect them all! Released on the 1st and 15th of each month.

SEVENTY
LIANA BROOKS

A Final Request for Mercy
AMY LAURENS

the kitten psychologist
vs.
the kitten's owners
THEA VAN DIEPEN

Answer the Question
AMY LAURENS

Happily, Red
AMY LAURENS

the kitten psychologist
tries to be patient
through email
THEA VAN DIEPEN

DRAGON
TUESDAY
AMY LAURENS

RED PLANET
REFUGEES
LIANA BROOKS

the kitten psychologist vs.
What The Kitten Did
THEA VAN DIEPEN

INKLET #016
Cherry Blossom
AMY LAURENS

INKLET #017
Alone
AMY LAURENS

INKLET #018
the kitten psychologist
& The Kitten
Come To A Conclusion
THEA VAN DIEPEN

INKLET #019
LEVEL NINE
LIANA BROOKS

INKLET #020
To Dust
AMY LAURENS

INKLET #021
Interchange
AMY LAURENS

INKLET #022
Emalia's Lanterns
LIANA BROOKS

INKLET #023
Dear Santa
AMY LAURENS

INKLET #024
The Quilt-Maker's Scrap
AMY LAURENS